JONNY BRIGGS
AND THE
GREAT RAZZLE DAZZLE

"My dog Razzle's the cleverest pet in the world!"
said Jonny Briggs to his friend Pam.

But when he gets home he discovers his best gold
belt is all chewed up, as well as Albert's sports bag
and Humph's astronomy book, and it very much
looks as though Razzle is to blame . . .

JONNY BRIGGS
and the
GREAT RAZZLE DAZZLE

Joan Eadington

Illustrated by William Marshall

as told in Jackanory by
Bernard Holley

 KNIGHT/BBC

I

Jonny Briggs had just had the best day at school he could ever have dreamed of: Miss Broom hadn't even shouted at him once; the twins had given him half an orange wax crayon which had been his in the first place, and Mr Badger the headmaster had actually sent him on a message! This meant something very special because Jonny knew that Mr Badger only sent people on messages when they understood what he was talking about.

He had seen Jonny outside the classroom and he said: "Jonny Briggs – take this message in to Miss Broom." He had handed Jonny a large piece of white paper with typing on it, and smiled very slightly with a quarter of his mouth and never even mentioned untied shoelaces or black finger-nails.

Then, to cap all this heaven, even the message turned out to be good because Miss Broom was smiling when she read it out: "The school is going to have a Clever Pets Show," she said. "It will cost everyone ten pence to enter and there will be prizes. All the money will be sent to the Save the Children Fund. I wonder if our class will win? Has anyone got any clever pets?"

Jonny put his hand up straight away, but he was completely lost in a forest of waving arms and sounds of barking, miaowing, clucking and cheeping. The Brown brothers swanked loudly about a frog that could jump over the television set – except it happened to be a battery worked one, from the market.

Then Nadine said *their* cat could run up the curtains, and Lily Spencer, whose mother was a nurse, said that her pet rabbit was *very* clever – but she didn't want it to catch anything from scruffy animals with fleas. And everyone gasped. And even Miss Broom coughed and said "Ahem" – and told them they could all go home two minutes early.

"Clever pets!" said Jonny to his friend Pamela Dean as they went home from school the long way round through the park, because it was such a nice sunny day. "My dog Razzle's the cleverest pet in the world! I'll bet he could win every prize there is." He looked at Pam excitedly – his fair bristly hair almost jumping off his head at the thought.

Pam looked at him enviously. She had her best white socks on and her hair was all brown and gleamy in the sun – and she was wearing Jonny's favourite plastic butterflies to fasten the bunches.

"I wish I had a pet," she said. "The last pet we had was Stew's grass snake. And it frightened mum so much we had to let it go – even though grass snakes don't harm anybody."

"You can share Razzle with me, if you want," said Jonny cheerfully. "We can meet here in the park – at the First Aid hut near the swings – and we can teach

6

Razzle some of the best tricks ever! So that he's better than anyone else's pet in the whole school."

Pam's eyes widened. She was as excited as Jonny. "That dog that followed you to Whitby and barks three times whenever your Albert says 'We are the Champions'?"

Jonny nodded blissfully.

"What a good idea, Jonny! Let's both get home

quickly and have our teas. Then come back here with Razzle."

So Pam went home through the South Road gate of the park where the houses with front gardens and privet hedges were, and Jonny went out at the gate by the boating pool near where Port Street was and hurried back to the door with the toffee on the door handle and J.B. scratched on the doorstep.

The house was quiet and peaceful. No one was back from work or school, and he smiled happily to himself.

He was just going to wander into the backyard to Razzle's kennel when Albert came flying in like a pinwheel on fireworks night – whizzing round and flinging books, clothes and bun crumbs in all directions.

Then Albert flopped flat on the floor and closed his eyes and said casually: "There's a shock for you in our bedroom. . . . And don't blame *me*."

"A shock, Albert?" Jonny's heart started to thud. His happiness level was sinking like a cooling thermometer: "How do you know if you've only just got in?"

"I haven't," said Albert, "I took one look and went back out again to buy a bun." Albert's face was a mixture of pretending-to-be-asleep looks – to see what effect he was having. And he certainly *was* having an effect because Jonny's thoughts were racing now as he imagined all the worst things that could have happened – like the window being smashed

with a football or mam chucking everything out in a
mad clean-up.

He dashed upstairs – and for the first time he did
two stairs at a time without even noticing. Then he
swung open the bedroom door. At first he thought
that Sandra, who was good at cooking, must have
been practising with her new mincer – because everything seemed to be in shreds. . . .

In the middle of it all, in a place of honour on the
remains of the peg rug, was his gold belt. His own
carefully-made gold belt – now carefully *un*made. It
lay there all chewed up at one end, looking as if an
army of starving mice had just had their first banquet
in a hundred years.

Albert had crept up behind Jonny. "It's not only your belt," complained Albert, "there's my Puma sports bag. And just look at *that!*" He pointed a bony finger at Humph's *Best Book of Astronomy*. All the corners had been chewed off.

"Something must have been *desperately* hungry to eat that!" said Albert meaningly. "A round scruffy black and white thing if you ask me." Then he rushed back downstairs and lovingly lifted the bread-bin lid and stuffed three slices of bread in his mouth.

Jonny was so dazed he hardly heard Rita come clattering up the stairs. "What are you standing there for all of a gawp? Are you waiting for a train?"

Then she stopped and stared into the bedroom. Straight away she saw the chewed-up gold belt and Jonny's face all miserable, and his eyes all watery.

"It's your own fault, our Jonny. Razzle's done that to your belt. It's your own fault for letting him in the house when we're all out. I don't blame that dog at all. It would be a nice intelligent dog if it had nice intelligent people to look after it all the time – like me and my friend Mavis."

Then she added: "That dog has potential. But it won't show its potential if it's shut up in this poky place all day while we're out!"

Jonny had a vague idea that "potential" meant that even Rita thought Razzle was a clever dog. But what was the use of all that now, if he was just going to use his potential chewing up the whole of the house, instead of being well-behaved and properly

trained to do really good tricks and be the top dog of all the pets in the school?

"But we don't leave Razzle in the house, our Rita," said Jonny. "He stays in the backyard in his kennel and old Mrs Foster keeps her eye on him. And Humph always comes home from school and talks to him at dinner-times."

Rita gave him a withering look and flounced away. Then she let out a huge shriek: "My best Zandra Rhodes model dress that Mavis made. Ow . . . Ow . . . Oow!" (It sounded like the end of the world.) "The slit's in ribbons! My *green* one. My *best* one! Chewed and dribbled on by that horrible animal!"

Jonny felt his "fading" feeling coming on. The weak, pale feeling that Rita's temper caused. Without waiting to hear another squawk he ran downstairs and out into the backyard to Razzle's kennel.

Razzle was sitting there quietly. He jumped up and wagged his tail when he saw Jonny, and his one black ear seemed to say "hello" all on its own.

Then Jonny saw something unusual in the kennel. It was a small glinting scrap of gold metal. A fragment of gold belt. Jonny picked it up and stared at it sadly. There was no doubt about it then . . . Razzle was the culprit.

Jonny began to puzzle out what he could do. Up to now, things had chugged away fairly smoothly – and even mam on her very worst busy days hadn't complained about Razzle. Now it would be different. If it had just been his belt it wouldn't have been so bad . . . but Rita and Albert were the snag. Albert always made the worst of everything – he thrived on trouble. And as for Rita – she was more dangerous still because she was good at arguing and talking and creating a big fuss. Humph was the only one who could outwit her. But Humph didn't spend his *life* outwitting Rita – there were better things to do!

Jonny went back into the house. He was dreading tea-time now, and mam and dad getting back from work. All that change in only half an hour! All that change from a quick happy tea and into the park with Razzle to meet Pam . . . to this! Tea-times were awful if there was trouble in the air, because with him being the youngest he never managed to say as much as the others and they never took much notice of him – except Humph, or dad when he was in a good temper.

But it didn't look as if dad would be in a good temper tonight. He hated trouble from Rita when he was eating mashed potatoes, and feeling tired.

Miserably, Jonny mooched about as mam came rushing in with eight mince-'n'onion pies which she put in the oven to keep warm. Eight pies . . . *that* meant that all the family would be there (except for Marilyn). It meant that Pat wouldn't have gone off to the ice-skating, and that Sandra wouldn't have gone to Marilyn's. And instead, all of them would be sitting there munching mince-'n'-onion pies and talking with their mouths full about *his* dog Razzle, and how it should be got rid of immediately . . . if not before . . .

Jonny could see it all!

Mam was in a cheerful mood when she came in. Mr Boulter, the new owner of the ironmonger's shop where she worked, had given them all a rise, and she and dad were saving up to have an extra bit built on the back of the house. Just a little bit – but a little bit which mam said would make all the difference as far as bedrooms were concerned. So she was even *laughing* and telling everyone about a little boy who came into the shop and asked for a tin of Elbow Grease. And when Jonny asked what it was she kissed him and patted his head.

Even dad seemed quite chirpy because Boro's manager had decided not to sell a star player after all, but do exactly what dad said he should do when he, dad, was talking to the lads in the pub last night.

"What's our Rita wittering on about?" said dad good-humouredly as they all tucked in to potato croquettes, pie and peas, and Arctic Swiss Roll. "It's amazing how you manage to say so much and eat at the same time, miss. What's happened to all that crisp bread and those dandelion leaves?"

"You've not been listening to a word, dad!" gabbled Rita. "I've just been telling everybody that that dog of our Jonny's has got worms . . ."

"Worms?" Mam's face went a yellowy shade. Things like that made her go all funny inside.

Jonny felt funny inside, too. Now it was all going to start . . .

Everyone stopped eating.

"It's chewed up my best green dress," said Rita wearily like a tired old lady of ninety-nine. "Mavis and I spent *hours* putting the slits in those dresses."

"When all you needed was to let Razzle do it," said Humph cheerily as he saw Jonny's fearful, tense face. "Never mind, our Rita – frayed ends and ribbon shreds will be coming in this year. The Chewed-To-Ribbons look."

"That's *not* funny, Humphrey," said mam, glaring at his wrinkled monkey face, sharply.

Then her eyes went all soft as she looked towards Rita again: "I know just how you feel, dear. You have a lot to put up with from those boys. It's a crying shame about that dress. If Mavis's Aunty Connie hadn't raked it out of her trunk in the first place – it could have cost you pounds . . ."

"It wasn't raked out of a trunk, mother!" said Rita angrily. (She always called mam "mother" when she was being extra sarcastic.) "Mavis *made* it for me."

"And *you* left it draped over my bed near the door just where the dog could get at it . . ." said Sandra, giving her a gingery glare.

"I never leave my ice-skating skirts all over the place," said Pat. "And stop talking about worms at tea-time!"

"Yes, I expect it will be full of long curling *worms*," said Albert, pretending to be deaf. "All the worms will be eating all the food inside it. It'll be starving. It must be – to eat an old gold belt! Next door's cat had worms. Big whopping tapeworms they were, like wriggling bands of white tape, and it was sick . . . and this long wriggling white thing . . ."

"*Shut up*, Albert!" bellowed mam in agony as three people left the table clutching their stomachs.

"There's no need to have hysterics . . ." said dad, unperturbed by any amount of wriggling gruesomeness as he got on with his tea – leaving the plate almost as shiny as when he'd started, and giving Jonny a big wink. "There's worse things in life than a dog with worms. All you've got to do is *deworm* it. And seeing as it's your animal, our Jonny, I suggest you take it along to the People's Dispensary for Sick Animals and have it checked up on . . ."

"In case it hasn't got worms at all?" said Jonny eagerly.

"Of course it's got them," snapped Rita. "That's why it's chewed everything up. They always do that when they've got worms!"

"But you said it was because it was in the house on its own. P'raps it was lonely, our Rita."

"Shut up – and do what dad says, Jonny," said Albert smugly while he pushed the remains of two partially eaten mince-'n'-onion pies onto his own plate, "otherwise it will eat everything in the house. The chairs, the beds – everything. And it will go mad and rush round in circles chasing its tail. And in the end it will have chewed the black bits of its tail right off. I'm not kidding either."

"So it chewed your gold belt did it, lad?" said dad, ignoring Albert. "Don't worry too much. I can get a bit more of that gold stuff. All you need to do is to cut the chewed bit off and sew on a bit extra. It'll make it last longer than ever." And dad's eyes sparkled and looked like mam's best tea-cups again.

So tea-time hadn't been so bad after all, thought Jonny! He would take Razzle to the dispensary first thing in the morning. Lots of people took their pets there when they'd swallowed glass marbles or had been trapped in the vacuum cleaner.

Then he remembered something – school! And something else – Pam in the park! He dashed off to tell her what had happened.

2

"Where's Razzle?" said Pam, when Jonny reached the First-Aid hut in the park.

Jonny looked down at the bare patches in the grass miserably. . . . In the distance the music from the roller-skating rink played carefree tunes as people swirled along on the smooth, concrete rink. And there were carefree people on the boating lake, too. And ducks quacking happily. And the fountain spraying carefree water in the flower gardens. It should have been a perfect summer evening. But it wasn't.

"Razzle's got worms," said Jonny.

"Worms?" Pam looked quite startled.

"Yes, he's chewed everything up – even my gold belt. Dad's told me to take him to the Dispensary for Sick Animals in the morning."

"What about the pet show then? What about the tricks? Won't he be able to do any?"

"Only chewing up things," said Jonny. "Just imagine if we took him to school and he chewed up all the class registers. . . ." Jonny's face brightened slightly as the thought sank in.

"Or Miss Broom's yellow custard-coloured cardigan," said Pam, giggling. "Perhaps it would taste of custard and he'd eat it all."

"Or Mr Hobbs' grey and black check pullover," said Jonny starting to laugh. "Just imagine Mr Hobbs without *that!*"

"He'd have to wear Miss Broom's yellow cardigan instead," said Pam.

"He couldn't, because it's chewed up –"

"And Miss Broom could wear Mr Hobbs' grey and black check pullover . . ."

"She couldn't because it's chewed up!"

And they both started to roll on the grass and do head-over-heels.

Then Pam said: "What time will you be taking Razzle then?"

"Early in the morning," said Jonny, "before he chews up anything else. Or even dad might get mad."

"But you'll be late for school. And you know what Mr Badger said . . . He said all people who were always being late for school would be too late to be allowed to take part in the pet show."

"I'll *have* to . . ." said Jonny, shaking his head. "I'll just have to take him – whatever happens." Then he smiled: "I know – if I'm not there – tell Miss Broom you think I've got a sore throat."

Pam nodded helpfully. "Shall I tell her you might be having your tonsils out? It'd make it sound more real."

Jonny nodded. Then he said: "Race you to the fountain."

And after that they went round sniffing all the

flowers and they bent down so low that Jonny fell flat
on a bed of velvety, rust coloured wall-flowers and
they both got told to clear off by the Parky.

That night in bed, Jonny couldn't get to sleep –
even though Albert had thrown off all the bedclothes
except the sheet, and even though Humph – who was
growing bigger and bigger every day – had decided to
sleep on the floor on top of his sleeping bag.

"It's better than having you wriggling about –
chucking all the clothes about, Albert," he said.
"And it's no worse than camping."

"Quite right," said Albert – spreading himself out
and jabbing Jonny as usual with his toe-nails. "Lots

of people in hospitals sleep on wooden boards. It's good for their backs. Mr Prince across the road once had to sleep on a wooden board . . ."

"Cut it out, Albert. Or I'll shift *you* here. And I'll get in *there.*"

Albert gave a loud snore, and said no more.

But still Jonny couldn't settle. School . . . he was supposed to go straight to school. If mam thought for one instant he wasn't going straight to school she'd be on to him like a load of bricks – just like she was with Albert when he'd tried to skive off!

"Don't expect *me* to write you any excuse notes, our Albert," she'd say. "And if that School Attendance Officer comes round – don't expect *me* to make excuses about you being off with a bad cold. You've never been off school as far as I know in your life . . ."

It was all very well for dad to say *take Razzle to be seen to* . . . Just as if you waved a magic wand. He probably thought that you just took dogs to the dispensary after tea at night, or on Saturday mornings.

There was another thing too. You had to put something in the box. They had a small wooden moneybox and the Brown brothers said that even *they* once put something in it. He remembered them taking their tortoise when it got glued up.

"And I haven't even a penny!" said Jonny all of a sudden in a very loud voice, sitting up in bed.

"Neither have I," said Humph's voice from the floor. "Lie down, our Jonny, and stop talking in your sleep."

The next morning everyone was up early.

"What a sweltering night," said Albert, "I never slept a wink. Our Jonny was babbling away all night. Something about money-boxes. Isn't there any toast? Haven't you made any toast, our mam? You know I like toast."

Dad was on the late shift that day, but he'd already been out in the yard to look at his cabbages. He was sitting next to Jonny. It was one of *those* meals again. One of those *everyone there* meals.

Jonny tried to talk to dad in a sort of secret way, but it was hopeless. "Dad . . ."

"Yes, son?" said dad, wiping the remains of a very nice fried egg off his plate with a bit of bread and butter and taking a satisfying gulp from a mug of strong, sweet tea.

"It's about taking Razzle, dad."

"Oh aye?" said dad. "He looks in quite good shape

this morning. Sat in his kennel good as gold. Little blighter! Keeps that great Sylvester away from the cabbages anyway . . ."

"Dad, when I take him . . . I might have to go this morning," said Jonny quickly. "And there'll be this money-box, dad."

Albert heard the last bit immediately.

"Money-box. Again, our Jonny?"

"I hope nobody's wanting money," shouted mam from the kitchen. "There's none of that due again till the school dinners next Monday."

"I've got thousands of pounds pocket money owing to me, dad," said Albert. "Thousands – ever since I was born."

"And" – Jonny suddenly felt a violent poke in his ribs – "I need enough money to buy another dress after your dog savaged my other one," said Rita, glaring.

"If that dog's going to start costing *money*," said mam, dashing in and plonking two bits of toast on Albert's plate, "we'll have to get rid of it." Then she said in a sort of kind voice: "P'raps we should take it to that vet who sees to all the unwanted animals . . ."

"Look, love," said dad, seeing Jonny's horror-stricken face for the first time, "let's be reasonable. Even *that* would cost at least four pints of best bitter."

And after all that, dad finished his breakfast and went off down the street to borrow a spanner.

And Jonny was left – with things just as bad as ever.

"What's the matter love?" said mam later, as she was dashing out to work, as if all the breakfast talk had never happened. "Now just you see you aren't late for school – you seem to be being extra slow. Aren't you going to finish off those cornflakes?"

Jonny smiled bleakly. Then mam gave him a sharp peck of a kiss and went. A minute later the door slammed twice and two more people had gone, until in the end there was only Jonny left in the house. And – at that very moment a stupendous idea came into his head – like a bright balloon floating in a grey sky except that the balloon looked like a very flat and battered box. An *Albert* box . . . Quickly, Jonny fetched the box, then went into the backyard to take Razzle out of his kennel. Then he gave Razzle the left-over cornflakes, got Razzle's new red lead from the kitchen, fastened it to his collar and set off.

Razzle's tail wagged like anything. It was strange, he just did not seem like a dog that went round chewing things up. . . .

Jonny had to walk very carefully with the large flat box under his arm. It was tied with a piece of straggly grey string and the cardboard was all soft and floppy and the red and black bits were wearing off the top of the lid. It was Albert's old Monopoly game.

It had suddenly dawned on Jonny at that moment when he was alone in the house that Albert had stopped playing Monopoly at least a year ago when some of the paper money and half the Chance cards slipped down an old chair that went to a jumble sale.

And so the Monopoly had stayed gathering dust under lots of other old games and comics.

But it wasn't going to gather dust any longer – because Jonny knew two people who always wanted things other people had got. Two people who might even have twenty-five pence each to give him for a Monopoly set if they did without crunchy chocolate nut bars and fizzy ice-creams for half an hour. Which would give *him* fifty pence to put in the money-box when he took Razzle to the animal dispensary. Those two people were the twins, Jinnie and Josie.

Jonny was just going towards the school gates and was standing on the pavement outside holding his

large flat box, with Razzle on the lead – when he saw Pam.

She stared in wonder. Then she said in a secret whisper: "I thought you said you were going to *the place*?"

Jonny's forehead wrinkled a bit: "I was. But I need some money. You're supposed to give them something. They say you shouldn't have pets if you can't afford to look after them when they're ill. So I'm going to try and sell our Albert's old Monopoly – then I can take the money."

"Your Albert's?" said Pam. "He'll KILL you!"

Jonny felt a few hairs stand on end at the back of his neck. "He never plays with it . . . and some of the bits are missing. And he's always trying to pinch my stuff."

"Nobody'll buy it with bits missing," said Pam.

"The twins might. They gave me those coloured pencils for my birthday with all the best colours missing . . ."

No sooner had he spoken than who should come sidling up to him but Josie. "What you got there, Jonny Briggs? Have you pinched it?" She pushed her round pink cheeks into a huge fat balloon and then exploded into a giggle which sprayed on to Jonny.

"Stop spitting at me, YOU," he said. Then he remembered that she was supposed to be his customer so he'd better try and be nice.

Then Jinny came running up, as well. "Is that Jonny Briggs spitting at you, Josie? Shall I go and tell someone? What's that big box, Jonny Briggs?"

"I only show it to special people . . ."

"Special?"

"Special people like *friends* . . ."

"We're friends," said Josie, trying to tug it from under his arm. "We came to your birthday . . ."

"It's a special game. And I'm going to sell it for fifty pence."

"Sell it?" Jinny and Josie looked at him with a sudden look of respect.

"What is it Jonny? Who are you going to sell it to?"

"It's a very special Monopoly game. They cost pounds in the shops. And they're not such thick cardboard as this one. That's why it'll cost fifty pence."

"*Fifty pence?*" Josie looked quite serious now. "Mr Badger's the only person with that much . . ."

"And you and Jinny . . ." said Jonny casually, as he and Pam gave each other a sly look.

"Us? We only get five pence a week, each!"

"You big liars," said Pam indignantly. "You stuff yourselves with Smarties and Mars bars all day long!"

"We never! It was just one day – when our Gran bought us some sweets."

"It never was!" Pam pointed a finger' at Josie. "You're even sucking a mint humbug *now*."

Jonny's spirits began to sink. The school yard was beginning to fill up and he was no nearer selling Albert's Monopoly set . . .

"And what've you brought your daft dog to school for?" said Jinny, looking at Razzle. "It isn't the pet show today."

"He's not bringing it to school," said Pam, putting out her tongue. "He's taking –" She stopped suddenly.

"You mean he's not coming in to school?" said Josie. "What will Miss Broom say?"

"He's got a sore throat," said Pam quickly, "haven't you Jonny?"

Jonny nodded.

"Ooooh err . . ." yelled the twins running into the yard. "Keep away from us! Jonny Briggs is covered in spots. Jonny Briggs has got bunions . . . Jonny Briggs has got pickled onions growing out of his ears! Jonny Briggs is daft and potty and made of treacle toffee."

It was too much. Within seconds, Jonny had rushed into the yard after them, forgetting all about Albert's Monopoly set as it fell on to the grey stone yard and broke open at one end, leaving Peter – who had been watching – to pick it up. Jonny galloped after the twins with Razzle barking furiously at his side and children scattering in all directions with screams and shrieks. (Things were always more exciting with a few screams and shrieks.)

And then at last Jonny thought he had them both trapped between the dustbins and a heap of coke, but they managed to dart away and into the girls' toilets.

"I'll report you to Miss Broom!" shouted the puffing red-faced Josie. "You've got no right to chase girls. And you've no right to spread sore throat germs."

"I don't care," grinned Jonny scornfully. "I'll keep you prisoners – till you say that it's you that's daft and potty and greedy and guzzling!"

"We never are! And you're a mean bully, Jonny Briggs," said Josie. "We'll tell on you, pinching that game and trying to sell it. *And* for not coming to school."

"And we'll tell on you for frightening everyone with that scruffy dog," said Jinny.

"It is *not* scruffy."

"It is! And it's savage – like a wolf – and dangerous – like a tiger –"

Razzle sat down and wagged his tail at this.

"It's you two that's savage and dangerous! You always start it."

"We never!"

A small neat boy came running up behind Jonny. "The whistle's gone. They're going in." It was Peter.

In a flash the twins had disappeared.

"Is this yours?" said Peter, handing Jonny the Monopoly set.

"It is, but I don't want it," said Jonny. "I've got to take Razzle to the People's Dispensary for Sick Animals, and I can't carry that as well. Don't tell Miss Broom though – about me not going in with the rest."

Then he said: "Will you look after it for me, Peter? You can have it if you like, but there's some bits missing . . ."

"Have it?" Peter's eyes lit up, and he nodded. "I'll give you ten pence if you want . . ."

Jonny's face glowed: "Will you?"

Peter put his hand in his pocket and pulled out a silvery ten-pence piece. "I've always wanted a Monopoly set. So I'll use this week's spends on it." And he hurried off – clutching the box, while Jonny rushed back towards the school gate with Razzle, praying that he wouldn't be seen by any of the teachers.

But now he felt happy again. And at least he had something for the money-box!

The People's Dispensary for Sick Animals was in a row of small shops in the middle of the town. The big glass window was painted cream with PDSA written on it. It was quite full when Jonny arrived with Razzle. There were old ladies with cats wrapped in bits of blanket, and a man in blue overalls with a huge Alsatian, and a little baby in a pram with a bird cage resting on top of her legs.

When it was Jonny's turn to go in he took Razzle into the back room. It was all white, like a hospital, with a wash-basin and a table and silver instruments and big bottles and jars. There was a man looking a bit like dad in a white coat. On top of a cupboard near the door was the PDSA money-box with a picture of some pets on it. Jonny clutched his ten-pence piece thankfully.

"So what can we do for you, sonny?" said the man.

"It's Razzle. He's got worms. . . ."

"Worms eh? Let's have him up on this table to have a good look."

Carefully, Jonny lifted Razzle's warm hairy little body on to the table. He was quite a weight . . . about as heavy as the special bag of washing mam sometimes took to the launderette. But Jonny was proud of Razzle as he stood there under the bright light – he was so trusting and well-behaved and so still that Jonny knew he could have balanced a feather on his nose and it wouldn't have moved.

Then Jonny told the man all about the chewed things – including his gold belt – and the man wrote down Razzle's name and description in a big diary, and when Jonny said his actual name, Razzle, and told the man it had two Z's in it, Razzle closed his eyes very slowly – then opened them wide again in a sort of big wink.

"He's a very nice, healthy little dog," said the man at last, after he had looked in Razzle's mouth, lifted up his tail, felt his tummy, inspected his paws and

studied his legs. "I can't see any sign of worms or any other ailment. But, bearing in mind what you've told me I'll give him a dose of some special medicine. That should do the trick. And if you have any more trouble with him chewing things – just bring him back and we'll see what else can be done. But somehow I don't think you'll need to worry."

Then the man patted Razzle and within minutes Jonny and Razzle were outside in the street again and it was all over.

It wasn't until Jonny was nearly home again that he remembered something.

"I never put the money in the money-box after all! And the man in the white coat never said. . . . P'raps if I take Razzle again I'll put it in. But I hope I don't have to take him again, because of the Clever Pets Show . . ."

Jonny began to think of school again. No good going back now, or the pet show would have gone for ever. They always *said* it was better to be late than not go at all, but everyone knew that to be *really* late you had to have a good excuse like a tooth out or a very large bandage. He would just have to go round the back of the house and see if the back door was open and wait for Humph to come in. And if Humph *didn't* come in he'd probably have to spend the ten-pence piece on crisps.

Jonny was nearly at the yard door when he suddenly noticed Razzle's ears go all sharp and pricked up, his nose all up-in-the-air and sniffy, and his eyes all beady and excited. And when Jonny opened the door: "Come back, Razzle! What are you doing . . ."

Razzle had run in and was shouting *hello, hello, what a nice surprise to see you again.* (At least, that's what the barking sounded like to Jonny.) And there, standing in the middle of dad's cabbage patch, was a small creamy puppy with big stout furry paws and brown eyes. Jonny was amazed! He was even more amazed when Razzle let the puppy run in and out of his kennel.

Then Jonny heard a voice calling from the house, "What are *you* doing? Why aren't you at school? It was his married sister Marilyn. She was standing there in a bright red and white apron and her big round glasses.

"I had to take Razzle to the animal place. Our Rita said he's got worms . . ."

"Worms! Keep him away from Chummy, then. I don't want little Chummy getting them! We've only had him three days. He's a watch-dog. He's going to keep watch and guard me while Ivor's on shifts." (Ivor was Marilyn's husband.)

Jonny nodded. Chummy seemed very little for a watch-dog.

"I came yesterday afternoon with him as well," said Marilyn, "to bring mam the catalogue back. But there was no one in except your Razzle. If I'd known Razzle had *worms* . . ." she shuddered.

Then, Jonny suddenly began to think very hard. "Was Razzle in the house with you, Marilyn?"

"In the house? Certainly not! There was only little Chummy with me in the house."

"What was he doing?"

"What was he doing?" Marilyn frowned a bit behind her glasses. "You're very nosy all of a sudden. It's me that should be asking *you* what you're supposed to be doing! Shouldn't you have gone straight back to school? It hasn't taken you all morning to take that dog to the PDSA!"

Jonny bent down and picked up Chummy. He was really cuddly, and immediately he started to chew

the collar of Jonny's shirt: "Get off! Stop chewing me to shreds . . ." Jonny stopped. Then he stared at Chummy. "Is he always chewing things?"

Marilyn hurried away and pretended not to hear. "I've got to go back now. Tell mam that I'll order the summer frock on page six hundred and three. That one with the stripes. And tell our Rita she still owes me for that sun-tan lotion and the beach bag . . ."

"Did he chew anything yesterday . . . ?" said Jonny.

"Yesterday? Don't ask *me*!" I don't watch the poor little thing every second of its life! Oh yes, it did chew some old scrap. A bit of that gold stuff that dad once got. Yes, I was worried about that, he had some bits between his teeth when he ran out to play with your Razzle. You want to be more careful leaving bits like that about for a little puppy to choke on . . ." And with that Marilyn hurried off out without so much as a goodbye, dragging the reluctant Chummy, chewing at his lead, behind her.

Jonny felt like leaping into space!

"Yippee!" he yelled at the top of his voice as he ran back to Razzle. "Yippeeee! It *wasn't* you. You haven't got daft old worms! It was our Marilyn's puppy. It was Chummy the chewer. Chewing everything up. . . . Yippeeee!" He raced round the yard, with Razzle doing three-foot leaps and twirls in the air.

And they were still doing three-foot leaps and twirls when Humph came in with enough chips for all three of them . . . gooey chips, all soft and squashed together in the paper . . . all warm and succulent. . . .

And in between those mouthfuls of salt and vinegar paradise, Jonny told Humph exactly what had happened.

3

Miss Broom was marking the afternoon register. It was in alphabetical order.

Nadine's name was one of the first because her second name began with an "A" – it was Nadine Abeson.

Then Miss Broom got to the "B"s.

"Mary Bennet?"

"Yes, Miss."

"Peter Binns?"

"Yes, Miss."

"Nicola Bridewell?"

"Yes, Miss."

"*Jonny Briggs?*"

"Yes, Miss." His heart began to thump as Miss Broom suddenly looked up. She was wearing some new gold glasses – with only half a bit of glass, instead of proper round circles – and she was looking over the top of them at Jonny. "You didn't come to school this morning, Jonny Briggs – and you usually stay to school dinner don't you?"

"Yes, Miss."

"Have you brought a note from your parents?"

"Please Miss – I forgot . . ."

"What was the matter with you?" Miss Broom looked stern.

"Please Miss – I had a sore throat, Miss."

"Don't keep calling me *Miss*. My name is Miss *Broom*."

"I had a sore throat, Miss Broom – Miss."

And in a flash – two arms shot up. "He never had a sore throat, Miss!" said Josie in her loudest and most dramatic voice. "He chased me and Jinny behind the dustbins and kept us prisoners till it was time to come into school."

There was silence in the classroom. Everyone almost stopped breathing. Miss Broom took a deep, steady breath and her bust expanded about three inches: "Is this true, Jonny Briggs?"

There was dead silence.

"Did anyone else see Jonny Briggs in the yard before school started this morning?"

The silence continued.

"*And* he had a scruffy dog with him, too – it tried to bite us," added Jinny breathlessly as she turned and stared at Jonny.

"Stand up, Jonny Briggs," said Miss Broom, very slowly and quietly.

Jonny stood up. His face seemed to be going red and white in turns – and all the chips Humph had bought were churning up inside him.

"Now then: hands up anyone else who saw this boy in the school yard? *Was* he in the school yard this morning?"

There was a moment's more silence, then a small quiet voice from the back of the class said: "Yes,

Miss. He was in the school yard." It was Patricia. She was very quiet and very truthful.

"And who else saw him there?"

Slowly, a few hands went up.

"So, what do you have to say to *that*, Jonny Briggs? And why did Pam tell me you were away, having your tonsils out?"

By now, Jonny was desperate. How on earth could he get out of it all? Any second Miss Broom might lose her temper completely and send him to Mr Badger and that could mean *anything* . . . It could mean being made to stand up in front of the whole school . . . It could mean a letter being sent to his father . . . It could mean staying in at play-times. It *might* even mean The Slipper. For, yes – Mr Badger still kept a slipper to whack people with in the bottom drawer of his desk!

But above all, what it certainly would mean was that he wouldn't be able to enter for the Clever Pets Show!

"We're all waiting, Jonny Briggs. . . ."

Jonny looked up at Miss Broom's gold glasses. Peter was his only hope. The only reliable friend he had – except for Pam. But Peter had to say the *right thing*. It all depended on Peter!

"Please Miss – I had to bring Peter his brother's Monopoly set. His brother saw me and said Peter needed it to give to Mr Badger for the school games cupboard."

"He's lying, Miss!" squeaked Josie jumping on top

of her desk, and sitting there pointing her finger at him. "He was selling it! He'd pinched it and he was trying to sell it."

"I had *not* pinched it!" burst out Jonny at last, clenching his fists, almost ready to bash Josie on the head with a knock-out blow then and there.

"Get off that desk this minute, Josie – and be *quiet*!" rasped Miss Broom. "Now then, *Peter*. What happened?"

Peter stood up solemnly – his hair smooth and shining, his blue T-shirt looking like a dazzling clean-wash advertisement. "He did bring the Monopoly set, Miss Broom. I showed it to the others at play-time."

There was a murmur of relief, and a pleased rustling noise went round the class as everyone relaxed.

But Miss Broom hadn't relaxed. "Where is it now then?" she said – sounding like a real detective on the television.

"I left it behind in the hall. It's hidden behind the piano."

"But I thought it was for Mr Badger's games cupboard?"

Jonny hardly dared even to blink his eyes as he waited to hear what Peter would say next. And, for what Peter *did* say next – Jonny blessed him all his life.

"It *is* for the games cupboard, Miss Broom. But there's some bits short. I wanted to check it first." Peter looked his neat careful self. Serious and thoughtful.

Miss Broom frowned a trifle suspiciously – but she had the rest of the register to do. She said no more – except to Jonny: "I shall expect a proper note about your sore throat first thing tomorrow, Jonny Briggs – or you go straight to Mr Badger!"

Jonny flopped down in to his desk seat like a quivering jelly. And when they started to do writing, his hand was quite trembly.

Then, towards the end of the afternoon – when everything was calm and sunny again and even the twins were quiet for once – and busy weaving their table mats, Miss Broom said: "Has anyone brought their entry fee for the Clever Pets Show?"

Lots of hands went up and there was a chink of money. And a long queue formed at Miss Broom's table as she took the names.

"Nadine Abeson – one black and white cat called Fluffy. Trick: champion climber, up anything.

"The Brown brothers – two fleas in a matchbox ..." (Miss Broom disqualified these immediately and they said they'd bring a rabbit that could blow a whistle instead.)

And so the list went on ... with clever dogs, cats, goldfish, budgerigars, hamsters, grasshoppers, earthworms, snails, two hens, and even a pony, until Miss Broom had filled a page with writing and a tin with money.

But Jonny's name wasn't on the page. He didn't dare mention Razzle after all that fuss earlier on. He didn't want it to start up again with those twins nattering on. They could ruin his chances in the show for ever! So he kept quiet.

But on the way home from school that afternoon he said to Pam: "We can beat that lot hollow with Razzle! He can do twirls and three-foot leaps in the air *and* he can jump through a hoop, and catch a sausage on the end of his nose ..."

"And don't forget 'We Are The Champions' barking three times," said Pam. "P'raps we could teach him to do sums and add up like they do on the telly."

"Except you've got to be able to do the sums first yourself," said Jonny doubtfully. "But tonight we'll train him properly in the park. We really will."

And they did – with some very surprising results. ...

But before all those surprising results began to

happen, Jonny had to go home and tell everyone that Razzle hadn't got worms at all – which was a *good* thing. And he had to ask mam for a note to take to school in the morning. And somehow he sensed that *that* was not going to be a good thing at all. . . .

"Our Marilyn's puppy?" said mam in amazement, when Jonny began to tell her everything: "I never even knew she'd got one! And you mean to say – she brought it yesterday as well as today when she came with the catalogue? What's it like – Jonny love?"

"It's a creamy colour with big stout paws, and it *chews* everything," said Jonny.

"Bless its little cotton socks," said mam, looking all romantic.

"Never mind going all soppy, our mam," said Rita sharply. "Just because it's our Marilyn's puppy and she paid the earth for it – doesn't mean it wasn't to blame for all the damage. You can just tell our Marilyn that I've *no intention* of paying for that sun-tan lotion and beach-bag after what her silly little toy of a puppy has done to my best dress! And tell her never to bring it to this house again!"

"Rita, how can you be so nasty –" said mam beseechingly. "The things our Marilyn does for you . . . the trouble she goes to –"

"The trouble her puppy gets *into*, you mean," said Humph, giving Jonny a knowing look. "And poor old Jonny having to trail Razzle all the way into the town to have him checked up."

46

Mam stopped pouring the tea: "Checked up? When did he do all that?"

"Dad told me to take him," said Jonny. "I went this morning."

"He didn't tell you to take time off school!" said mam accusingly. She had gone all bristly and grumpy. For some reason the thought of any of them sneaking off school was like a red rag to a bull! She was always going on about education being important and telling them to make the best of it and grab every chance – whatever that meant – when they almost *chained* you to school in the first place.

"It was the best time to go," said Jonny.

"It certainly was *not* the best time to go," said mam.

"Never mind him, mam," said Albert who for some reason was busy practising standing on his head with his legs leaning against the living-room wall. "I want to get round to Tommy Wilton's dead quick."

"You're going a funny way about it then," said Humph.

"Get away from my wall immediately with those awful muddy shoes!" said mam.

Albert slowly and calmly brought a pair of thin stringy legs down to the solid earth. "We're starting a Monopoly League. There's this big whopping competition held in London. It's a final play-off of all the players of Monopoly – all over the world – and Tommy Wilton, and me are going to put the bits of both our sets together to make a decent one – and we're starting this league."

Jonny could hardly believe his ears. Not *now?* Not at this very worst – most complicated – moment after all the time it had lain in a heap, covered with dust. He began to wonder whether Albert was a mind-reader who somehow *knew* the most troublesome time to start making some new and complicated trouble. . . .

"I shall need a note for school in the morning, mam," said Jonny hastily – feeling that even the trouble over a note would be far, far better than even a breath of trouble over Albert's Monopoly.

"A *note*, our Jonny? You're getting no notes from me – my laddo!" said mam in an acid voice. "It wasn't me that told you to stay off school this morning. If it was dad who told you to take the dog – then it's him who can write the note," and mam crashed about getting the tea ready with great angry bangs.

Jonny groaned. "Please let it be one of dad's favourite teas," he said to himself: "And please – *please* not fish with bones in!"

And when he did come in at last – with the *Evening Gazette* under his arm – Jonny prayed that the Boro wouldn't be in it – sunning themselves on a seaside beach abroad, because dad would get all tetchy and start chuntering on about them not getting enough serious practice in and he would be in a bad mood for things like notes for the teacher.

But Jonny was lucky. Mam had actually given dad

his favourite meat pie with an egg in the middle, and the *Gazette* was full of Yorkshire winning the cricket match.

"Please dad – could you write me a note to take to school in the morning – saying I've had a sore throat?"

"Sore throat, son?" said dad looking up from his paper. "What did the doctor say it was then?"

"I didn't go to the doctor. I took Razzle to the dispensary – like I've just been telling you . . ."

"So you haven't got a sore throat then?" said dad stopping dead half-way through the pie as he tried to fathom out Razzle and the worms, and a strange tale about Marilyn's new puppy – all mixed up with trying to work out the batting averages of the Yorkshire cricket team.

"I had to *tell* them I'd got a sore throat, dad."

"But that's lies, son. Lies'll get you nowhere."

"It is a *bit* sore," said Jonny, rubbing the front of his neck and giving a painful gulp. And it was true. It was a bit sore – due to a very sharp potato crisp scratching as it went down, when he swallowed the extra big curly one with the razor edge that Pam had given him.

"Bring us some paper then, and let's get it over with," said dad, sighing. Then he said: "Why can't mam do it?"

"Because it's nothing to do with me," said mam, quick as a flash. "He should never have stayed off in the first place."

"What's the teacher's name then?" said dad, getting out his pen. "Brush was it . . . Besom . . . Sweeper . . . ?"

"Miss Broom, dad –"

"Broom – ah that's it. And how do you spell it?" said dad scratching his ear.

"It's got an 'O' in it said Albert cheerfully: "B-R-O-M."

"Aren't you getting muddled up with West Brom – our Albert?" said Humph.

"Oh, shut up, Mastermind!" said Albert. "It's got two 'O's in it, if you want to be fussy. I was just testing. And it'll all be done with computers soon anyway. All you'll need to do is to just *talk* and it'll come out on the paper properly spelt. Fancy worrying about daft old spelling!"

"Get out, Albert!" said dad. "I need to concentrate."

Then he wrote:

Dear Miss Broom,
Please excuse my sun Jonny being away.
He had a sore throat.
Yours Faithfully,

Then dad looked very sly and his eyes sparkled a bit and he wrote *Dad* in big letters at the end.

"You can't put *Dad* on a letter to the teacher," gasped Jonny, almost in tears. "She'll think I've written it!"

"She will, judging by the spelling," said Humph. "It should be son . . . not *sun*. The sun is what shines in the sky."

"And our Jonny's going to shine like the sun one of these days – aren't you laddy?" And dad patted him on the shoulder.

Then he said: "I'm not altering it!" But he did write his proper grown-up name as well. Then he smiled and said, "If she doesn't like it – tell her to send it back, and I'll come and see her personally." Then dad put the note in an envelope and handed it to Jonny. "If that doesn't satisfy them nothing will," he said. "And now let's have a bit of peace."

So they let him have some.

Jonny got out of the house as soon as he could after that. The house was about the most dangerous spot in the whole world now that Albert was looking for his missing Monopoly set. So he took Razzle and went to the park to meet Pam.

As soon as they were within the park gates he undid Razzle's lead and watched him racing along joyously on the broad stretches of grass.

But as they got near to the boating pool Jonny noticed something very strange happening. The ducks were all squawking like anything; they were flapping about and leaping in the air and doing mad flutters as if they were trying to escape.

And all the people on the boating pool were crouching down as if they were going to be hit by ducks any minute. And the man on the loudspeaker was saying: "Keep calm, boat thirty-three. They aren't going to *eat* you."

There were thin black metal railings round the edge of the pool, and there was an island in the middle of it where all the ducks lived. Usually they were very happy and just swam about – quacking and clucking – and even having games with the boats that zoomed near them, but on this summer evening there was something seriously wrong.

Jonny and Razzle stood and watched, while Jonny tried to puzzle out exactly what it was. . . .

4

Jonny and Razzle had only been standing there a few moments when something else happened.

The ducks stopped just leaping about and squawking, and about eight brown ones with greeny-blue heads and white bands round their necks rose into the air and flew high above the railings straight to some big trees where all the grass was.

And then who should Jonny see but Albert and his latest crony Tommy Wilton! Tommy Wilton was big and hefty and wore a blue denim jacket with *Tommy* written on the back with metal studs. And they were both running towards the boats.

Then, to Jonny's amazement, Albert – who only had on shorts with frayed edges and a skinny coming-undone T-shirt – jumped into the boating pool and started to do a sort of dog-paddle across to the island in the middle, while Tommy Wilton shouted: "It's stuck in those brambles – next to that green bush!"

And after that, all hell was let loose! The man from the boating pool hut where you paid your money came out waving his arms and roaring his head off then scrambled into a motor-boat and shot across to the island. . . . Someone else still in the hut was going berserk on the loud-speaker, bawling and shouting to that stupid idiot of a kid to get out of the pool immediately (with a whole stream of four-letter words at the end, of the very rude sort)!

Jonny stood frozen to the spot. It was like being in a horror film, with Albert being in it. It was much worse when someone in your own family was being chased.

He watched panic-stricken as people in small boats got out of the way of the motor-boat and sat there with their mouths wide open waiting to see what would happen next. Jonny had visions of Albert being dragged by his hair to the local police station, mam having a quiet weep over her toast in the kitchen, and dad having to do without pints of Best Bitter for months in order to bail him out – like they did on the Westerns with Albert sharing a cell with cowboys. *And* a crooked sheriff with a silver star on his big black hat, who shared the cell, offering Albert a swig of illegal liquor out of a flask – whereupon Albert would collapse on the floor – because that was what happened to people who drank stuff when they were too young!

The only people who didn't seem to have been impressed were thirteen boys and two girls fishing round the side railings. They just put their jam-jars and keep-nets away and slunk off home grumbling and groaning and saying fishing in town parks was a dead loss.

Then – just as the motor-boat got to the island – up popped Albert himself from the bushes – all muddy

and covered with slime and dead leaves and bits of crisp-bag paper and shreds of plastic.

And he was holding . . . .

Jonny blinked to make sure . . . yes, he was holding a magnificent, modern, shining model aeroplane. It had wide slender wings and was bright orange and silver. And Jonny could see straight away that it was one of those expensive ones worked by remote control. And as it – *no way* – belonged to Albert Briggs – Jonny guessed it must be Tommy Wilton's.

Then the man in the motor-boat grabbed Albert and pulled him into the boat, and they zoomed back towards the hut again.

Jonny didn't stop there any longer. There was enough of his own trouble in the world without getting mixed up in Albert's. So he hurried towards the First-Aid to see Pam.

For some reason Pam had a disappointed look on her face: "Didn't you bring him after all?" she asked.

Jonny frowned: "Bring who?"

"Razzle of course!"

Jonny gaped at her as it slowly dawned – Razzle! Razzle wasn't here any more. He must have slipped away to enjoy himself whilst all that fuss was going on.

"He can't be far away," said Jonny looking round desperately. "He was here only a minute ago."

Then he told Pam all about Albert and the aeroplane on the island: "It must have been the plane landing that frightened all the ducks."

Pam nodded, wide-eyed. "Fancy your Albert swimming in there to get it. I hope there was no glass! He must be very brave . . ."

"The man on the loud-speaker said he was very *stupid*," said Jonny mournfully: "I hope our mam doesn't hear about it. She's always saying that Tommy Wilton makes a mug of our Albert by getting him to do all the dirty work. And you should have *seen* Albert this time! Phew . . . I'll bet he pongs!"

Just then they heard a whole lot of quacking coming from the trees and stretches of grass. "Hadn't we better go and see if Razzle's over there?" asked Pam.

Jonny nodded half-heartedly. He was feeling hot and tired now. His old grey cotton shirt was clinging to his shoulders with sweat, and suddenly the whole world felt a dusty, mucky place with Albert – and trouble – right in the middle of it all!

Nothing ever seemed to work out how you wanted it. Here was he – about ten minutes ago – happy at last – with Razzle in the park, ready to teach him some nice peaceful tricks – and with Pam to help him. And now – instead of all that goodness – it had changed to Albert and that big thing – Tommy Wilton – causing havoc in the duck-pond – and Razzle – gone for ever . . .

"There he is!" shouted Pam suddenly, as she started to run towards a small animal with one black ear and a black spot on its tail.

Then she stopped and said: "And just *look* what he's doing!"

As they hurried towards the grass, Jonny noticed that a whole lot of other people had wandered in the same direction – and now there was quite a big circle of men, women and children, standing, watching, smiling and pointing. And in the middle of them all was Razzle . . . and eight ducks! Ducks with white feathers and big bright beaks and white chubby necks – all quacking and walking in a group – while Razzle ran round them in circles keeping them in order.

"What a clever little dog!" said an old lady who looked like the Brown brothers' granny. "Is it from a circus?"

"No," said a plump lady with four children next to her, "it's part of the Summer Entertainments run by the Parks Department."

"It's the police dog. The mascot from Dundas Street," boomed a big voice from the back. "The little dog with the big brain. It belongs to the Chief!"

Jonny walked up to Razzle: "It's mine!" he said.

"Yes, it's his," said Pam, standing by his side as Razzle kept running round the ducks.

"You want to hang on to him, lad," said someone. "You've got something good there!"

And a few moments later the boating-pool man came hurrying towards them. It was the one who'd hauled Albert off the island.

Jonny took a deep breath and pretended not to notice. After all, the man didn't know that he – Jonny Briggs – had seen the duck trouble in the first place

and that Albert was his brother. . . .

Then he saw that the boating-pool man was actually *smiling* at him. "Good work, lad," he said looking at the ducks.

Then he turned to a tall man with a camera round his neck who was with him and said: "Aye, the ducks and the kids would make a very good photo, Arthur. It would be a good bit of publicity against vandalism."

"That tall one's from the *Gazette*, Jonny," said Pam excitedly. "He once took a picture of Stew playing footy. We might be in the paper tomorrow!"

"See if you can get your little dog to work the ducks back to the pond," said the man.

Gradually, Jonny and Pam coaxed Razzle in the direction of the boating pool again, and – sure enough – Razzle kept all the ducks together in a little

waddling, quacking group – just like a sheep dog with sheep, until at last they were back to the pool next to the ticket hut and boat landing stage. And – as easy as wink – all the ducks quacked and flapped themselves on to the water again!

Everyone was beside themselves with wonder and amazement at Razzle's fantastic performance, but he just stood there calmly wagging his tail.

"I've never seen owt like it since they had that top dog show in Stewarts Park!" said the man who used the rude words on the loud-speaker ... (At least Jonny *thought* he had ...)

"I think you deserve a little something for helping us like this, sonny," said the other man smiling. "How would you like a free fishing pass?"

Then it dawned on Jonny just what he *would* like. It was the only possible happiness-making thing. ...

"Was it that plane that frightened the ducks?" he asked.

The men looked grim, and the motor-boat one said: "It was more than that. It was some big lads. Some hooligans."

Jonny looked at Pam, then he looked down at the ground and scraped his sandal in a wet patch on the ground. "Had one of them got floppy black hair and bony elbows?"

"Aye, he was a bit like that, son. I've taken his name and address – I'll have to report him."

"He lives down our street," said Jonny breathlessly.

Then the man read out: "Donald Duckson, sixty-nine, Graft Street. Is that the one?"

Pam was just going to say it was the wrong name and address – when she felt Jonny's sandal press her shoe. "I'd sooner you didn't report him than have the free fishing ticket," said Jonny.

"Oh aye?"

Then Pam said helpfully: "His mam'n' dad'll beat the living daylights out of him."

The man frowned and Jonny could see he just didn't quite believe *that* bit.

"He once rescued me from some deep water," said Jonny.

And at this the man's face softened and all the lines on it melted away. "P'raps there's more to 'im than meets the eye," he said, grudgingly, and before Jonny and Pam's very eyes, he took the page from the notebook with Albert's false name and address on and ripped it to shreds.

A bit later when Jonny, Pam and Razzle were feeling all happy again and they were about to go home through the different park gates, Pam said: "I didn't know Albert ever *rescued* you Jonny? Was it *very* deep water?"

Jonny sighed and scratched his head. Then he said: "It was our bath. Our Albert dragged me out of it last week because *he* wanted to go in and just because I yelled at him – he told our mam he'd rescued me from some very deep water."

"Brothers are awful," said Pam.

And Jonny agreed. Then he ran off back home with Razzle.

When he got in, all Albert's clothes were hanging on the line in the yard.

"And thank goodness *you* aren't all covered with mud and slime as well!" chuntered mam. "Our Albert must have been mad to get in that state!"

Jonny went into the kitchen and got a drink of water. He would have *liked* to have told everyone about Razzle and the ducks. But he didn't dare – or it would have all come out about Albert as well. So he went straight upstairs to bed and read comics until Albert came into the bedroom. And then he pretended to be asleep because Albert was turning the place upside down hunting for his Monopoly set.

"It *was* here," he kept saying. "It was here only

three days ago! I remember seeing it. Someone's moved it. Just wait till I see our mam. If she's chucked it out – I'll. . . ." And he went out of the room muttering and fuming.

And the last thing Jonny heard before he fell asleep for the night was a great buzz of commotion going on downstairs with sudden loud voices and bits of conversation batting at his ear-drums – like: "I NEVER TOUCHED IT!" and "HAVE YOU LOOKED IN THE WASH-HOUSE?" then a few bits of quietness and a loud: "IS IT UNDER THE CHAIR IN THE FRONT ROOM?" . . . Then a loud clattering and slamming of doors and "OH – GO TO BLAZES!" Then: "WHAT ABOUT OUR JONNY – HAS HE GOT IT?"

But by now Jonny was too sleepy to care, and he fell asleep dreaming of Razzle and the way he dazzled everyone with his cleverness.

5

"Please mam," said Jonny the next day, "can I have ten p. for school?"

"Not *again?*" groaned mam, as she hastily ironed two T-shirts. "What's the excuse this time?"

"That show at school, you know . . . (*the times Jonny had to tell people things. You could tell mam things a million times and she never remembered!*) The Clever Pets Show – tomorrow in the school hall. Tomorrow afternoon at two o'clock. You can come an' all if you want; parents and everybody. It'll cost you ten pence as well. Our Razzle'll be in it . . . if you've got ten pence, our mam . . ."

Reluctantly, mam hunted in her purse. "No change, love. Ask your dad."

"But he *never* has any change – ever." Jonny's face fell a mile. "It's for a good cause, our mam. It's for Save the Children and I'll bet anything our Razzle'll win it!"

"Very well," said mam with a glimmer of a smile. "But it should be Save the Mothers if you ask me!" Then she gave him ten pence without another murmur – except to say that she'd see if she could get half an hour off work, just to pop in and see it all. And Jonny was more delighted by that bit of news than all the rest. It was much nicer having your own parents at school than being left there without any; with only the twins' mother fussing round, and Lily Spencer's mother looking at everyone else's work to see if it was as good as Lily's. And Peter's mam giving him, Jonny, a sweet because she felt sorry for him.

Jonny seemed to be at school in two minutes that day. "We can enter it!" he yelled, as soon as he saw Pam in the school yard. And Pam waved her arms in the air, and the twins pulled faces at her and said that

she and Jonny Briggs wouldn't win because clever pets had to have clever owners to train them and Jonny Briggs's head was made of solid wood.

"From the *tree* of knowledge . . . Nair!" retorted Jonny jubilantly.

"From the *board* of education . . . Nair!" bellowed Pam boisterously – because she liked having shouting matches with Jinny and Josie.

Then both she and Jonny chanted: "Sticks and Stones may break my bones . . ." right to the end, and gave pop-eyed squinting Monster grins with thumbs on their noses while they ran to line up in the yard – because by then the whistle to go in had gone.

Jonny was next to Peter as they went into school: "About that old Monopoly set, Pete," whispered Jonny. "Can you get it back? I never used your ten pence to take Razzle to the dispensary – so here's your money . . . Albert wants the set back."

But Peter shook his head: "You'll never get it back now," he said with sadness and alarm. "It's in Mr Badger's Quiet Games cupboard – and he's written it on the list inside the cupboard door. He seemed really pleased to get it. If you take it out of there he'll be telling the whole school it's been stolen."

On the way to the classroom Jonny kept trying to think what he could do to get that Monopoly set back. Somehow he felt there was trouble brewing over it. He felt in his bones that Albert would not rest until he'd found out exactly where it had gone. And the thought made him very uneasy. If only he could get it back out of Mr Badger's cupboard . . . but how . . .?

Then as they went into the classroom he forgot about it because so many other things were happening and everyone was talking about tomorrow's pet show – and at last he was able to see Razzle's name put on the long list of clever pets when Miss Broom put his money in the tin.

"And what sort of tricks does he do?" said Miss Broom with her pen poised over a column headed TRICKS.

"Please Miss, he rounds ducks up."

"Rounds ducks up?" said Miss Broom putting down her pen very quickly and looking like she did on the school outing when a thunderstorm was due: "I don't think he'll be able to round ducks up in our school hall, Jonny Briggs!"

"He can do six-foot leaps and twirls as well," mumbled Jonny. And he saw Miss Broom write: jumps and twirls (without the six-foot part).

That morning after prayers in the hall, Mr Badger made an announcement. "The response to our show has been extremely good," he said. "We will be having a well-known vet to do the judging. All the animals must be under proper control and in suitable containers. Large animals, such as dogs, must be looked after in the bicycle sheds. We can't have them all running round mad in the hall. All pets and pet owners must form a queue and answer to their names when they are called to perform their special trick and – seeing that there are eighty entries – no trick must last longer than half a minute. Mr Hobbs will be the time-keeper and will ring the school gong every half-minute."

Then Mr Badger cleared his throat slightly and said: "There will be a small prize for the winner and perhaps a few other *very* small prizes. For, as you all know, it's the thought that counts and not the prize."

The rest of that day it was absolute bliss at school because the teachers were all busy getting ready for tomorrow and there were extra long play-times, and Miss Broom kept on receiving messages from Mr Hobbs and leaving them all to "get on, on their own". And at one time even Jonny Briggs was allowed to go and help move all the chairs in the hall and put them ready for everyone to watch the show.

On the way home that afternoon Jonny felt as if he was in a real adventure. And he sailed along the streets as if he were on a massive tree-trunk being swept along a huge river in Canada – like they'd seen on the Saturday morning film and every so often he gave a leap in the air as he leapt on to special paving stones and was swept along safely through the tor-rents . . .

Then he reached his own front door at Port Street and the dream stopped. Because he could hear real life going on. And real life was still Albert nagging and worrying about his wretched Monopoly set. "It can't have just 'vanished'," Albert was saying to Rita. "I'll swear someone's been up to something."

"Well, it's no good going on at me," said Rita as she slung a couple of college books on to a chair and went to gaze in the mirror. "I never did like Monopoly anyway . . . Mavis and I are going to hitch-hike to Mongolia with two Geology students who work for British Rail."

Jonny's heart leapt with sudden joy. So Rita was moving out at last! "When do you go, Rita? Will it be forever?"

Rita spun round: "Oh – it's *you*," she said. "No, I shall *not* be going for ever – more's the pity. Mavis and I can't go till these two Geology students save all their wages up . . ." Then she added in a slightly lower voice with a ring of annoyance in it: "And mine – the one with the curly hair and the strong arms and Geology hammer – well, he said it might not be as soon as Mavis and I had imagined because he's just bought a . . ." She stopped suddenly and said to Jonny: "Didn't I see *you* with Albert's Monopoly – our Jonny? Yes – I'll swear I did." Then she said slowly as her eyes bored into him like needles: "It was when Mavis and I were waiting for the bus and you were going to school with Razzle, and a big flat box. That box was our Albert's, now I come to think of it."

Jonny didn't wait a second longer. He shot out of the house and back down the street towards the paper shop where there were always lots of people about and where all the paper-lads waited with their bikes and delivery bags – for the packets of evening newspapers.

In a place like that he would be safe. But at home with the combination of Rita and Albert, Jonny knew it was what Humph would call *dynamite*.

So what could he do?

Then he had an idea. He decided to wait for dad, because dad always collected his paper from the shop on the way home when he wasn't on a late turn.

"Whatever's all this?" said dad when he came out of the paper shop with the *Evening Gazette* under his arm and saw Jonny.

"Just thought I'd come and meet you for a change, dad . . ." he said, a bit sheepishly.

Dad patted his head, and said nothing and they walked home together. And by the time they got in all the rest of the family were in, including mam, and Jonny felt safe again . . . because Albert had rushed off to tell Tommy Wilton his worst suspicions about the Monopoly set. But even so, Jonny knew that he'd have to have thought of something pretty good by bed-time, with him and Albert being in the same bed and Albert's toe nails never having been cut since the year dot. . . .

They had all settled down for tea and dad had just started to read the paper when he suddenly said in rather a pleased voice, "What's all this then?"

"All what?" said mam. "It's only the same sausages as we usually have . . . although I think they are a bit more meaty than usual . . ."

"Not *that*!" said dad turning away from his dinner plate. "I mean . . . *this*!" He showed the inside of the paper to mam.

"Glory be . . ." said mam in a daze. "It looks a bit like . . . a *bit* like . . ."

"It is!" said dad grinning delightedly. "It's Jonny and Razzle!"

And there, in a large photograph, was Jonny in the park, and some blurred things that were the ducks. But Razzle was *very* clear. And so was Jonny.

And he felt so shy at seeing his photograph in the

paper that he ran into the front room and crouched down behind a chair to wait for the fuss to die down.

Under the photo it said: A SUMMER WONDERLAND *A moment of pure magic captured by our ace photographer as dog performs circus act* . . .

"Circus act, eh?" said dad in wonderment.

"I expect they've got to put *something*," said Humph.

"Mmmm . . ." said Rita as she looked at it thoughtfully. "P'raps Mavis and I could send that paper to those other two Whitby ones we met on holiday. They always said that dog had potential. I wonder what happened to them . . . those other two?" And she went off down the road to meet Mavis, looking very thoughtful.

Later on that night things went even better for Jonny because Albert decided to stay the night at Tommy Wilton's and mam hastily agreed. So there was no night time Monopoly trouble after all . . . even though Jonny knew that something still had to be done to escape Albert's final onslaught.

"I wonder if I could wear my gold belt for the pet show tomorrow?" thought Jonny as he stood in the bedroom on his own – in one rare quiet moment of complete peace. "It's supposed to be for adventures and tomorrow with Razzle should be a really good one and my gold belt might bring us luck . . ."

He had never dared take it to school since he had first made it. But tomorrow would be different. It wouldn't be like real school – because everyone would be busy with pets instead of grabbing things off you.

So he went downstairs and did what dad had suggested. He cut off the chewed-up end of the gold belt with mam's big kitchen scissors, and got the fresh bit dad had given him and slowly stitched it on. It was *very* hard work, and he had to use a darning needle and thick thread. It was so hard to do, that sometimes he had to press the needle through the gold stuff with the back of an old wooden ruler of Humph's. But he sat there on his own at the kitchen table and gradually finished it – and in the end the belt was longer and even better than before. And he took it up to bed with him and put it proudly on top of the comics.

A bit later that night when mam and dad were having a cup of tea, dad said: "Our Jonny's a good little worker, when he feels like it."

"Aren't we all?" said mam. "When we *feel* like it."

Then they both laughed and mam said: "The trouble is he never seems to feel like work at the right time – according to Mr Badger at school. But he seems to have set his heart on that pet show tomorrow. He's worked very hard teaching Razzle to do jumps and twirls. In fact they've very nearly driven me stark raving mad at times."

And with that mam washed the tea-cups and she and dad went to bed as well.

Humph was still lying there dead to the world when

Jonny got up the next morning. Jonny knew it was going to be a very special day. It *must* be – because mam had slipped in last night and there was a freshly ironed shirt lying on the chair and a pair of clean blue jeans and a *new* pair of socks! When Jonny saw them he gave himself an extra good wash and combed his hair very carefully.

But when he crept downstairs mam had beaten him to it. She was already there, hurriedly drinking tea and putting the empty milk bottles out.

"Whatever's got into you our Jonny? You don't need to get up yet! It's different for me. I've got to get to the shop extra early today to make up for the bit of time I'm having off. Couldn't you sleep?"

"Yes, mam. I just thought I'd get up and get my own breakfast – like when people are camping."

Mam frowned. "I hope our Rita gives you enough breakfast whenever I go out early?"

Jonny didn't reply to that. "I only want cornflakes, and I want to get Razzle ready."

"All right then. But be a good boy. And good luck at the pet show. I'll keep a look out for you . . ." Then mam gave him a quick kiss and dashed off out.

As soon as she'd gone, Jonny went quietly into the backyard to get Razzle. He had an extra plan for Razzle this morning and that, really, was why he had got up so early. It was because he was going to give Razzle a very special bath. A bath fit for a star dog.

And a bath fit for a star dog meant using the proper bath – upstairs. "I should just be able to manage it," said Jonny to Razzle, "before the rest of them get up." So he left Razzle with a couple of Crunchy Dog biscuits to eat while he went upstairs to run the water.

"I mustn't make it too hot . . ." he thought. "And he won't need much." So he ran the water in and he squirted in some scenty bath essence that Rita had left there the night before.

Then he brought Razzle upstairs.

Razzle had never had a bath in a proper bathroom before. Usually he was washed outside in the yard in an old white enamel baby bath that mam used for everyone when they were babies.

But now it was all different as Jonny lifted Razzle into the proper bath – hugging him firmly to his stomach as he managed to tip him in.

Then Jonny began to rub Razzle all over with some Jasmine-scented toilet soap Pat had left there. Then he swilled him down with bath water saturated in Rita's essence of Midnight Sin which Razzle didn't seem to mind one bit, and gave his paws an extra good wipe with Sandra's face-cloth.

And all this time, Razzle was what is known as the *epitome* of good behaviour – and apart from splashing water on the walls and ceiling and wagging his tail vigorously and shaking himself once or twice – he never even uttered a squeak.

At least, not until Jonny pulled the plug out and started to dry him on the big blue bath towel while Razzle was still in the bath. Then – as this turned out to be very awkward – Jonny lifted Razzle on to the bath mat to finish drying him.

It was then that Razzle was unable to contain himself any longer as he let out a volley of excited yelps and did a gigantic leap in the air – sweeping the towel on to the window-ledge where it dislodged dad's shaving foam, six tooth-brushes and a bottle of pink gargle mixture. Then he rushed out of the bathroom barking furiously, spreading perfume and pools of water all over the place.

Pat was the first of the girls to appear (she always got up first because of going to work at the chemist's). "My God!" she said, and hurried back into the bedroom to report to the other two.

Then Jonny heard Sandra shriek: "It will have got next to my *face*-cloth. I'll need to sterilise that face-cloth now! I'll need to boil it in salted water for at least thirty minutes as a safety precaution!"

Then Jonny heard Rita gradually waking up to it all: "In the bathroom?" she was saying blearily. Then she woke up properly and said, "I can smell my best Midnight Sin – all over the place!" And she thumped out of bed like a horde of mad buffaloes and chomped out of the room and tripped over the bath towel which was now lying in a soggy lump on the landing.

Jonny fled for his life!

In no time at all he had whipped Razzle's new red collar and lead out of the kitchen and was half-way to school. Even though he was an hour too early anything was better than that lot!

When he reached the school gates, Mr Box the school caretaker was only just opening them. "What's up?" he said. "Couldn't you sleep?" Then he looked down at Razzle and rubbed a finger underneath his old black tank beret and said: "I thought pets wasn't till this afternoon?"

"Yes," said Jonny, "but I stay to school dinner,

and I've got him all specially nice and clean. Something might happen if I left him till this afternoon."

Then Jonny told Mr Box all about Razzle and his early-morning bath and Mr Box said: "Oh aye? Well there are folks as don't like dogs sharing their washing arrangements – and I don't blame 'em." Then he added, "I see you've got your gold belt on . . ."

"Yes," said Jonny, pleased that he'd noticed.

"And your photo was in last night's paper? My, my, what is the world coming to?"

And Jonny went all shy and uncomfortable.

"I'll tell you what though," said Mr Box. "I'll look after that animal for you till this afternoon, if you like. He can stay with me in my room next to the boilers – because I'll bet you a penny to a pound that the teachers won't want animals scampering about too early – and neither shall I."

Reluctantly Jonny agreed to let Mr Box look after Razzle. But he didn't really want to. He just didn't want to let Razzle out of his sight until the pet show. He'd had visions of persuading Miss Broom to let him tie Razzle to the classroom desk for a while, and feed him on dog-biscuits to keep him quiet.

"Don't let him go and roll in the coke – will you Mr Box?" he called out anxiously as Mr Box went away.

"He won't go rolling in anything while he's with me . . ." said Mr Box.

And so, at last, the afternoon arrived.

"We're right next to the end of the list," said Pam. "We're number seventy-nine. I expect it's because we were late entering. The very last person to enter was Pauline Smith's hamster that eats baked bean labels. She nearly didn't enter it because her mother only had tinned spaghetti and it won't eat those."

"Have you got the hoop ready for Razzle to jump through?" said Jonny nervously. His mouth had gone all dry and yet his nose was sweating. Pam's nose was sweating too.

"Is anyone coming to watch?" she said, as they heard Mr Badger welcoming all the visitors who had now come into the hall and were sitting round on the chairs complete with shopping bags, babies, and small children.

"My dad's here – on his own," said Pam. "Our mam had to go and get her hair done, but dad's off sick with his toe in plaster."

"My mam's here," said Jonny, proudly. "I can see her on those chairs near Miss Broom."

Then Pam said to Jonny: "We've got the hoop –

but we've forgotten the most important thing – Razzle!"

Jonny's face had gone scarlet with panic as he rushed from the hall to Mr Box's room. He could hear the gong going like the clappers as people put pets through their paces: galloping goldfish, superior stick insects, candy-eating canaries. A pony that hopped, and pattern-making pigeons. *Doing, doing, doing* . . . every few seconds as they filed past the vet to perform the tricks, with a lady in a white overall – whom Jonny had never seen before, standing there with a mop and bucket in the background, and Mr

Badger putting ticks against the names of the pets on a big board as everyone kept clapping. People would have just finished one clap when – *doing* – the gong went and they started clapping again for the next one.

"Calm down," said Mr Box when he saw Jonny's puffing, panting, scarlet face. "The dog hasn't gone. I was just going to bring him across. He's eaten a whole block of chocolate since he's been with me. He's got a right sweet tooth. I don't really think he wants to move . . ."

"But he's *got* to," said Jonny anxiously, hoping

that the chocolate wouldn't make Razzle so lazy that he'd just sit there instead of doing the tricks.

"Go on with you, then. And p'raps I'll try and watch, if I have a few minutes to spare after cleaning up all the mess class four left in the wash-basins."

Jonny rushed back with Razzle and by the time he'd got safely back in the right position in the long line of performers they were up to – *doing, doing, doing* – seventy-two. The place seemed to be full of barking dogs and miaowing cats and the vet had lost a button off his coat, and the lady was busy with the mop and bucket.

At last – it was their turn!

He and Pam marched forward with Razzle to the seventy-ninth lot of claps.

Then Pam held the hoop and Razzle jumped forwards through it – then back again.

Then Jonny waggled his hand high in the air and Razzle did the most *amazingly* complicated jumps, twirls and four-foot leaps that had ever been seen in the history of the school! Everyone clapped themselves silly.

There was no doubt about it – Razzle was the champion! He was the out and out winner by even *world* standards, and poor Pauline Smith's hamster who only managed to nibble the edge of a baked beans label was left high and dry even though everyone gave her a good clap as well because by now the seats were getting a bit hard and people were getting fidgety and wanting to get home.

"Razzle *must* be the champ . . ." whispered Jonny to Pam with his eyes shining. And Pam smiled back and nodded.

Then all of a sudden, there was a lot of fuss all round Mr Badger's big board. And Jonny saw Mr Badger and the vet talking to Josie and Jinny and the Brown brothers.

It could only mean one thing . . . trouble!

And then they all turned and stared at Razzle. . . .

Then Mr Badger walked forward and spoke to everyone. "The first prize," he said, "goes to Maureen Thompson with her cat Columbus that shakes hands."

There was a murmur in the hall as if people were surprised. Then they all clapped again and Maureen went up to the vet who shook hands and gave her a present, a book entitled "Animal Care".

Jonny and Pam watched in a deflated and miserable daze, as second, third, and even fourth, fifth and sixth names were called out – plus ten consolation prizes as people went backwards and forwards to shake hands and receive bags of sweets and packets of foreign stamps with animals on. Gradually Jonny's eyes began to smart, and he had to blink to stop himself from crying.

And at that moment he heard Mr Badger say: "We

must at least mention the truly wonderful performance given by Jonny Briggs and Pam – and their dog. But protests were made because this is a circus animal and not an ordinary pet."

"It never *is*!" shouted Jonny indignantly – not caring if it was even the Manager of the England football team who'd just spoken. "He's not a circus dog, he's just *clever*. He's just an ordinary clever dog!"

Immediately the whole hall was filled with people talking and Jonny saw his mam making her way hurriedly towards Mr Badger and saying something.

Then Jonny noticed Mr Badger giving a quick sharp suspicious glance to where the twins and the Brown brothers were standing.

Then he said, as cool as a cucumber, "I think perhaps there has been a *slight* misunderstanding brought about by a photograph in last night's paper which described a certain animal as – performing a circus act. I am assured by Jonny Briggs's mother that the animal is not a circus animal and that it was just the way it was written in the paper."

Then Mr Badger coughed politely to Mrs Briggs and said, "And so we are giving a small extra prize to Razzle, the dazzling jumping dog, for his star performance." And Jonny saw the vet hastily take a fifty-pence piece out of his pocket as if he had made a mistake, and pop it into a fawn envelope which Mr Hobbs had rushed forward with.

"That is to share between all three of you," said the vet as he shook hands with Jonny.

"I should like a word with you – afterwards," said Mr Badger to Jonny . . . but he was smiling.

"Well, at least it was exciting," said Jonny to Pam as they watched everyone hurrying home.

"Thank goodness your mam was there," said Pam, "or we'd never have got a thing."

And Jonny felt a warm glow inside. Mothers could be quite good things to have – sometimes. . . .

"And now Jonny Briggs," said Mr Badger when everyone else had finally gone home: "I was wondering whether you would like another little gift – just to make up for all your disappointment . . ."

And on Mr Badger's desk was Albert's Monopoly set!

"I've a feeling," said Mr Badger, "that it belongs to the Briggs family in the first place. No – don't try to say anything. As you well know there are some bits missing so you're not getting much back. But your Albert might want to keep it after all – considering that his name is scrawled all over it inside the lid."

Inside the lid! He'd never ever thought of that. He'd never even looked inside, when he brought it to school! So Mr Badger must have found out the true story . . .

Without a word except an amazed "thank you", Jonny took the Monopoly set. Then he and Razzle went home at last, and he put the Monopoly set back exactly where it had been in the first place.

"What a performance at that Clever Pets Show!" said mam when she saw him. "It's a good job I was

there. There must be some right little devils in your class, our Jonny! I never thought there could be any worse than you at times! Protest indeed! The little demons!" Then mam started to laugh. "Just wait till I tell your dad. And as for Mr Badger – I think he thought I was going to clock him one!"

But Jonny never said anything. Mr Badger had

been very nice for once. Mr Badger had actually been fair to him, Jonny Briggs, and it seemed like a miracle.

"Oh yes . . . ?" said Albert glowering at Jonny at tea-time. "You've gone very quiet all of a sudden. Is it because of your Top Dog? Because if it is you'd better start thinking of something else – my MONOPOLY SET."

"Why, Albert?" said Jonny innocently. "The last time I saw it was five minutes ago in the place it's always in."

Albert rushed away to find out and came skulking back, carrying it. He scowled suspiciously and his head of floppy black hair got nearer and nearer to Jonny until they were nose to nose as Albert glared threateningly.

"That's enough Albert," said mam sharply. "For goodness sake leave the poor kid alone."

And Albert reluctantly decided to do just that.

"Back to another ordinary day," thought Jonny as he set off to school the next morning. But somehow it wasn't ordinary any more. It was ordinary for the rest of the Briggs family because they'd forgotten yesterday already.

But Jonny hadn't. And neither had Miss Broom.

"Today," said Miss Broom, "you can write about what happened at the pet show yesterday, and about all that money we made for the Save the Children Fund. I will put all the hard words on the board . . ."

and she took a piece of chalk – ready to chalk the words up.

"Please miss – how do you spell Razzle?" said a voice.

"How do you spell 'protest,' miss?" And "vet" and "circus" and . . . the list seemed never ending, and soon the blackboard was full.

But one person hadn't even noticed. He was writing and writing and writing. And *he* knew very well how to spell Razzle and circus.

And for the very first time he was writing and working like the clappers because he really wanted to! "School can be good – sometimes . . ." he said to Pam, and she nodded in happy agreement!